I love Mama. She cooks and cleans and plays with me every day.

On Saturdays she makes carrot pancakes for breakfast. I love carrot pancakes!

Mama Has Hyperemesis Gravidarum

(But Only for a While)

by Ashli McCall

illustrated by Anna-Maria Crum

To my children, Emmil and Elise, and to yours.
- AM

For Gail. A sister in truth as well as in law.
-AC

International Standard Book Numbers
ISBN: 1-4392-2367-X
ISBN: 9781439223673

Illustrations and book design by Anna-Maria Crum

Library of Congress Control Number: 2008912097

Today Daddy is home. He and Mama have a surprise: There is a baby in Mama's tummy. I am excited! Mama says she might get sick. Very sick. Daddy says that things might change a lot.

But only for a while.

We are very happy. Each day we talk about the baby. Is it a boy? Is it a girl? What will the baby's name be? It's fun to guess!

Saturday comes. I want carrot pancakes, but there are none. There are only Frosted Carrot Flakes instead. Mama is not at the table. Daddy says she isn't feeling well. She is still in bed.

It is dark in Mama's room, and she is very still.
I climb onto the bed for a hug, but she hops away to the bathroom. I hear her making scary noises. She is throwing up.

Mama stays in bed each day. She does not cook or clean or play. She does not eat or drink. She stays in her room and throws up. A lot. I am worried.

Daddy takes Mama to the doctor.
Grandma comes over to play.
She makes carrot pancakes, but they are not like Mama's.

Daddy comes home.
Where is Mama? She is
in the hospital. I miss her.

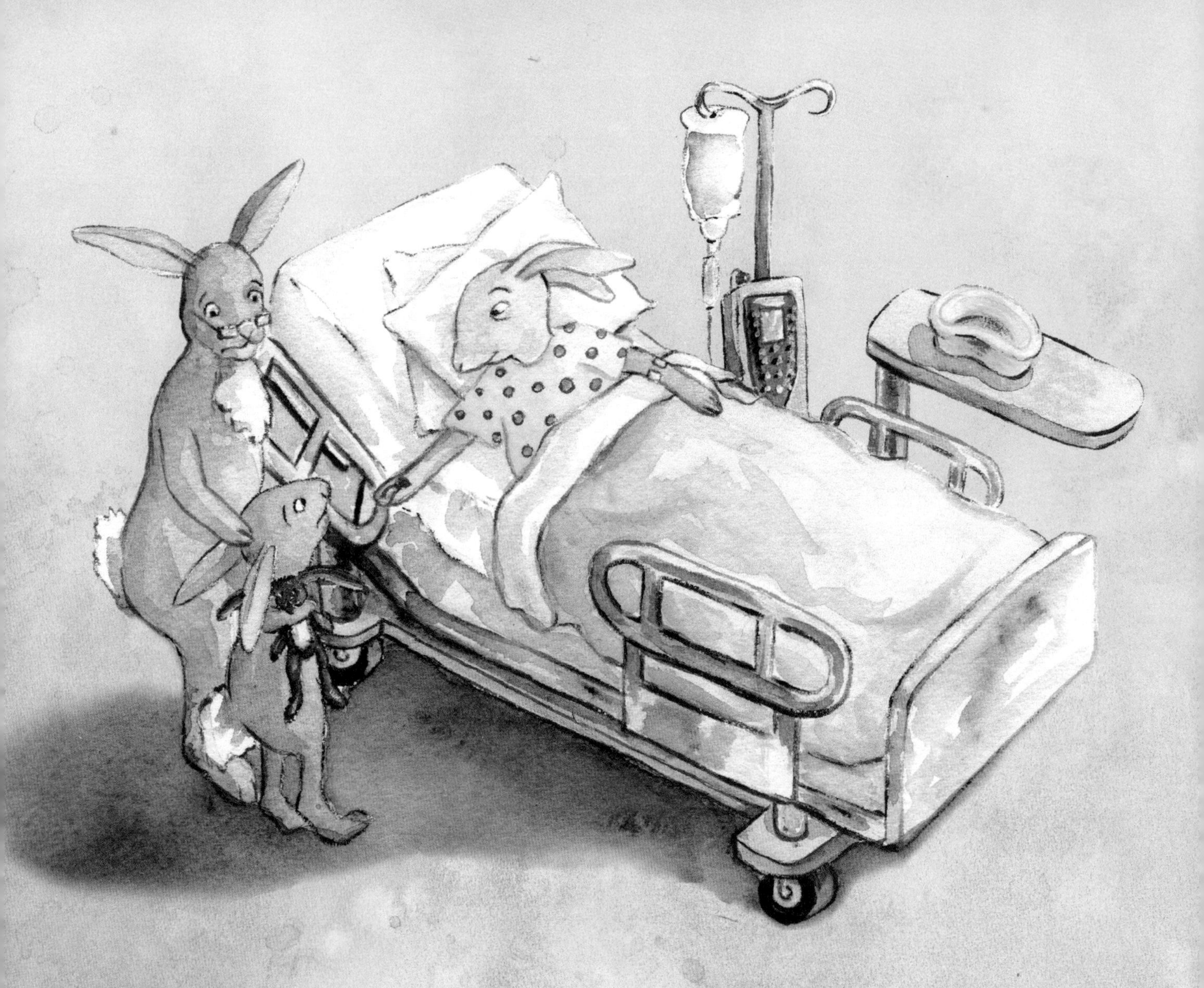

The hospital smells funny. It makes my nose scrumple up. Mama has a tube in her arm. It frightens me. Daddy says it gives her food and water. I want to go home.

Mama is home from the hospital. She still does not cook or clean or play. She throws up and cries. Sometimes she goes back to the hospital, but she always comes home. Today she doesn't want me in her room.

Does Mama still love me? Daddy says yes. He says Mama is sick. Very sick. But only for a while. It feels like forever.

Nurse Bunn
visits Mama.
She gives me a
glove balloon and smiles.

She pokes my mama,
and I see blood. Daddy
says she is helping.
I pop the balloon.
GO AWAY, Nurse Bunn!

Is Mama going to die? Daddy says no. He says she will just be sick. Very sick. But only for a while.

He takes me to a movie.

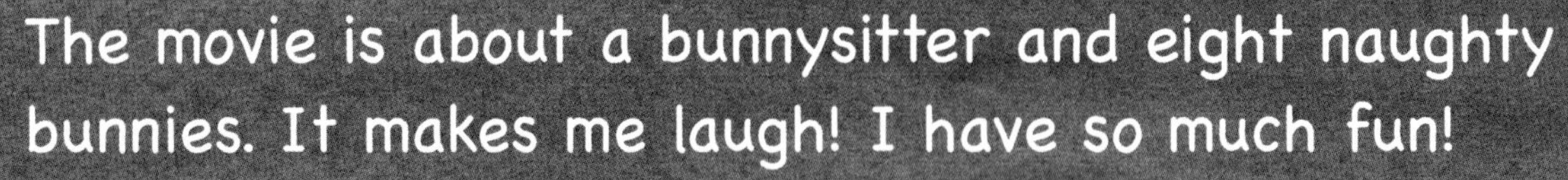

The movie is about a bunnysitter and eight naughty bunnies. It makes me laugh! I have so much fun!

The movie is over too soon. It is time to go home. When I throw my drink away the trash can smells yucky.

I gag. Mama has a trash can. She gags.

Trash cans are bad!
I kick this one.
Daddy gives me a hug
and takes me home.

Weeks go by. One Saturday I am eating Frosted Carrot Flakes for breakfast when...

Mama comes to the table! She does not eat. Instead she talks to me and smiles. I smile too!

Mama spends more time with me each day. Very slowly she begins to cook and clean and play. She sips carrot soup and cries. Daddy calls them cheerdrops, because they are happy tears.

Daddy takes Mama
to the doctor.
Grandma comes over
to play. Will Mama
come home
this time?

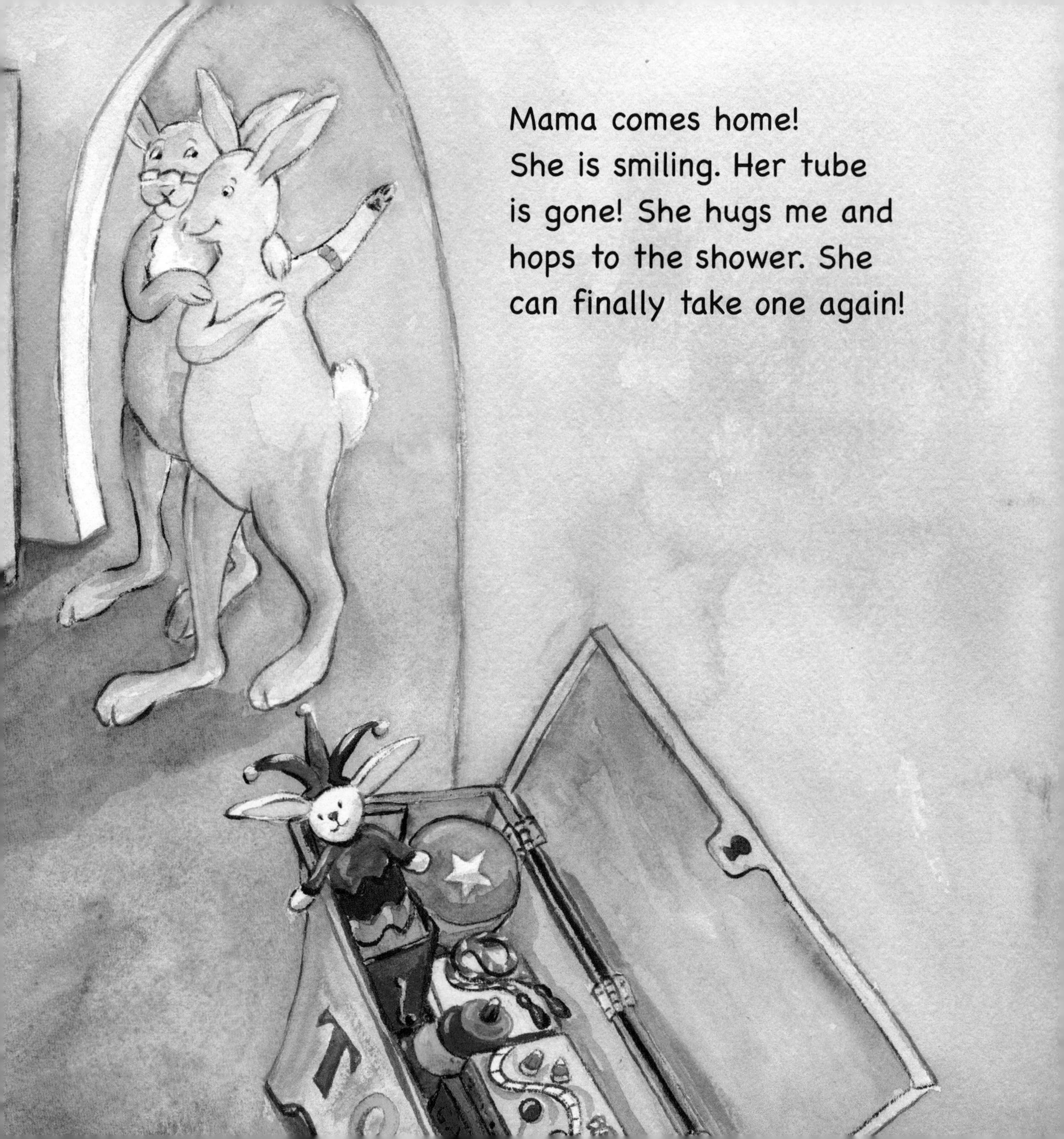

Mama comes home!
She is smiling. Her tube
is gone! She hugs me and
hops to the shower. She
can finally take one again!

On Saturday I help Mama
make carrot pancakes.

I’ve got my mama back!

We are very happy. Each day we talk about the baby. Is it a boy? Is it a girl? What will the baby's name be? It's fun to guess! It's hard to wait.

I want the baby to come out now!
Mama says I will have to be patient.
Very patient. But only for a while.

Printed in Great Britain
by Amazon